INKHEART™

MOVIE STORYBOOK

Adapted by Sonia Sander
From the screenplay by David Lindsay-Abaire
Based on the novel by Cornelia Funke

SCHOLASTIC INC.
New York   Toronto   London   Auckland   Sydney
Mexico City   New Delhi   Hong Kong   Buenos Aires

ISBN-13: 978-0-545-00706-1
ISBN-10: 0-545-00706-2

©2008 New Line Productions, Inc. All Rights Reserved. Inkheart™ and all related characters, places, names
and other indicia are trademarks of New Line Productions, Inc. All Rights Reserved.

Published by Scholastic Inc.
SCHOLASTIC and associated logos are trademarks and/or registered trademarks of Scholastic Inc.

12 11 10 9 8 7 6 5 4 3 2 1   9 10 11 12/0

Book design by Rick DeMonico and Heather Barber

First printing, January 2009

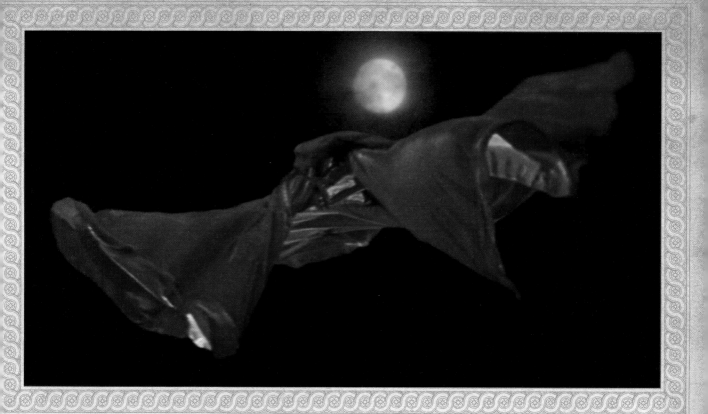

*Some storytellers can cast a spell over an
audience using just words. But other people
have an even more magical gift . . .*

esa Folchart was warm and cozy, sitting in front
of the fire, rocking her baby girl, Meggie. Her
husband, Mo, sat next to her. He was holding a
book: *Grimms' Fairy Tales.*

"Let me read to her," he said. "Once upon a time there
was a little girl. Her grandmother gave her a little hood of red
satin. The little girl wore it all the time and so she was called
Little Red Riding Hood."

Outside, unseen by anyone in the room, there was a flash of
red. A red satin cape floated lazily down from the sky.

Back inside, Resa reached for the baby's bottle that she'd
left on the windowsill, but it was gone.

Several years later

ou know I have a book report due tomorrow, right?" twelve-year-old Meggie reminded her father, Mo.

"This is the last one, I promise," he answered as they walked along a narrow cobbled street toward the Alpine Antiquarian Bookshop.

Mo traveled far and wide restoring old books. After her mother disappeared nine years before, Meggie always went with him.

Carts piled high with books lined the shop's entrance. Mo's fingers ran over the spines as he scanned the titles one by one.

"Maybe you'll find it here, Mo," said Meggie. "That book you're always looking for."

"What?" asked Mo, stopping abruptly. "I'm not looking for any particular—"

"Yes, you are," Meggie interrupted. "What, you don't think I've noticed? We never leave a bookstore until you've checked every corner, every shelf. You always come away disappointed."

As Mo headed inside the shop, he gave his usual warning, "Remember, no reading aloud."

Meggie nodded and rolled her eyes. Like she'd ever forget. She'd only heard her father's warning a thousand times.

 nside, Mo headed into the maze of shelves. Each shelf was crammed with old books. Just as he had done outside, Mo checked every title. He even lifted books, looking behind them as if he'd lost something. But there was nothing there.

Then, as he ran his fingers across yet another row of books, a strange thing happened—a trail of whispering voices floated into the air. Mo didn't seem surprised. Books had always whispered to him.

Suddenly, Mo stopped. He stood absolutely still. There was a new whisper—a woman's voice. He knew that voice. He headed in the direction of the voice.

After years of searching, he had finally found it—*Inkheart*. Mo didn't know if he should leap for joy or burst into tears.

utside, Meggie settled onto a bench with a book and a chocolate croissant. As she took a bite, she heard a chattering noise. Standing on its hind legs only a few feet in front of her was a small weasel-like creature. He was staring longingly at her food.

Meggie tore off a bit of croissant and tossed it to the animal. He gobbled it up. Another piece followed. And another. With each bit, he edged closer and closer to Meggie. When she got near enough, Meggie reached

out to tickle the animal under his chin. He whipped around, baring razor-sharp teeth and hissing loudly. Meggie gasped and jumped from the bench.

"He doesn't like to be tickled," called out a man who was leaning against a nearby light pole. "You should be more careful. His name's Gwin. He looks charming, but you know what they say about books and covers."

"Uh, yeah, I do," Meggie replied, edging away. "I also know what they say about talking to strangers. Excuse me . . ."

**J**ust then Mo walked out of the bookstore. "Hello, Silvertongue," the man said to Mo. "I was just having a little talk with your girl."

"Meggie, go to the van," Mo said sternly, and then calmly he added, "It's okay. He's . . . an old friend."

Meggie started to argue, but Mo ordered her to go. Meggie froze, then turned and ran off. Mo had never spoken to her like that.

"I've been looking for you," Dustfinger began.

"Tell me what you want," sighed Mo.

"The same thing you want. To undo the damage you did nine years ago," answered Dustfinger. "And I've come to warn you. Capricorn knows where you're staying. His men are there now. He wants you to read for him."

"Well, he's out of luck," insisted Mo. "I won't do it. If I ever do it again, it'll be for one reason and one reason only."

ustfinger tried to grab the copy of *Inkheart*, but Mo broke free and raced back to the van. As they sped away, Meggie grabbed her father's leather case. She had to know what Dustfinger wanted.

"No! Leave it alone!" Mo yelled, snatching the case away and tossing it into the backseat. "You're not allowed to even touch that book."

Mo refused to talk anymore as he drove south toward Italy, where Meggie's great-aunt lived.

Meggie's great-aunt Elinor lived in a mansion, behind an iron gate made of spear heads. Elinor seemed almost as friendly as that gate. But Mo told Meggie that she'd like Elinor eventually. Meggie wasn't so sure.

he next day, Meggie got up early. She wanted to explore the house. She wandered down a long hallway until she came to two tall doors. Pushing the doors open, she stepped into the most amazing room. Everywhere she looked there were books. Lots and lots of books.

In the center of the room was a display case with a glass top. Meggie crept closer and pressed her nose to the glass so she could see what was inside.

"Step away from the case!" a voice cried. It was Elinor. "What are you doing in here, child? This is not for children. Out! Out!"

"If I promised not to *touch* anything, could I just . . . sit and *read* in here for a while?" Meggie asked.

For a long moment Elinor stared at her. Then she turned and pulled something off a shelf. "There's a window seat overlooking the garden," she finally said. "That's where your mother would curl up." Elinor handed Meggie a book. It was *The Wonderful Wizard of Oz.*

With a final warning not to touch anything, Elinor swept out of the room.

Meggie curled up in the window seat, carefully opened the book to the first page, and began to read.

 he next night, Mo was working on Elinor's collection of books while Meggie sat in the library and read.

Thunder cracked and rain pelted the windows, but Mo barely noticed. Suddenly light filled his workspace. A fire was burning in the fireplace. Mo turned and found Dustfinger standing behind him.

"I tried to warn you," Dustfinger reminded him. "I gave you every opportunity to do this the right way. But you refused. All you had to do was read me back. You could've kept the book. But you ran off. I had to turn to Capricorn. He promised to help me."

The sound of breaking glass came from the library next door. Mo rushed in, but he was too late. Capricorn's men, led by Flatnose and Basta, were already tearing the library apart and burning every book in sight as they held Meggie and Elinor captive. Then they forced the three prisoners into a waiting van and drove them to Capricorn's village.

apricorn had Meggie, Mo, and Elinor locked in the stables. The other stalls were filled with strange creatures.

"Where did these monsters come from?!" Elinor demanded.

"Books," Mo said. "They were inside books. I've heard of others who could read them out, but I've never met one."

"Read them out? What do you mean?" asked Meggie.

"Meggie," began Mo. "This is the story you've been waiting to hear. We were house-sitting for Elinor. Me, you . . . and your mother, Resa. We had brought a couple of books along and one of them was *Inkheart*. It was a good read—adventure, magic, a mob of villains . . . and The Shadow—a creature so terrifying . . . I read several chapters aloud, and nothing happened. But then, my voice brought Dustfinger and Capricorn out of the book . . . your mother went in."

Meggie started to cry. "How do we know where she is? Or if she's even alive?" she asked.

Mo couldn't answer. All he could do was hug her.

 he next day, they were summoned to Capricorn's castle. The great hall was lit by thousands of candles. Black-jacketed men filled the room. Capricorn was sitting on a large throne.

"I won't read aloud," protested Mo. "Not with Meggie and Elinor in the room."

Capricorn ignored him. "Here's how this is going to work: You do whatever I say, or I'll kill the old lady and lock your daughter in the dungeon."

With that, he tossed Mo a book—*1001 Arabian Nights*. "It's a good one. Filled with riches," he said.

Mo began to read. The hot sun and sand of the desert filled the air, and a magical waterfall of gold coins rained down. Sacks of riches followed, and gems and pearls gathered in mounds around the room.

Suddenly a fifteen-year-old boy wearing a turban appeared, and one of Capricorn's men disappeared. Capricorn didn't seem to mind. He was only interested in the treasure.

t's my turn now," interrupted Dustfinger. "Like you promised."

"Your turn?" smirked Capricorn. He held up Mo's copy of *Inkheart*. "Ohhh, you mean this. . . ."

Capricorn glanced at the book once more, then smiled and tossed it into the fire.

"You promised I'd be sent back!" Dustfinger cried.

"Yes, I know," said Capricorn. "I lied when I said that. I'm a liar. I lie all the time! Lie, lie, lie! All these years, you think he would've figured it out by now."

Dustfinger dashed to the fire to retrieve the book. But all he did was burn his hands.

ustfinger retreated
to the kitchen.
One of the maids
tended his burns.
Dustfinger remembered when
she was read out of *Inkheart*.

The next morning Dustfinger
found one of the maid's drawings—it was
a picture of Mo and Meggie! Dustfinger realized that the maid was
Meggie's mother, Resa. She must have been read into the story the

same night he'd been read out. Later on, she'd been read out by one of Capricorn's less successful readers.

Dustfinger promised to help her escape and find her family. But first, he had to rescue Mo and Meggie.

o had his own plan. "My voice was different when I read! I was never so in control of it!" he said. "I know I can get Resa out of the book. And maybe send Capricorn back in. We just have to get another copy."

"I bet the author has a copy," said Meggie.

Just then, the door creaked open to reveal Dustfinger. "Before you say anything, just know that I'm here to save your necks," he said. "You want your wife back as much as I want to go home."

Dustfinger tossed Mo a copy of *The Wonderful Wizard of Oz*. Mo knew what he had to do. He started to read.

When the tornado hit, trees and chunks of roof flew through the air. The guards panicked and ran for cover. In the chaos, no one noticed as Dustfinger picked the locks, and Mo led them all away through the forest.

hey had finally reached a nearby town, but Elinor decided she had had enough. It was time to go home. "I prefer a story that has the good sense to stay on the page where it belongs. Take care and good luck," she said and left to catch a train.

Leaving Farid and Dustfinger in the town square, Mo and Meggie climbed up a hill to an apartment and rang the bell.

They were greeted by an impatient, elderly man in an apron—
Fenoglio, the author of *Inkheart*. Mo wasn't sure Fenoglio was going
to believe his story. He was right to be worried.

"It's a good story, I'll give you that," Fenoglio said. "Silvertongues.
Great concept. I wish I'd thought of it! But it's too absurd to take
seriously. I know my characters are so lifelike that they seem to jump
off the page, but it's simply not possible."

o and Meggie had no choice but to take Fenoglio to see Dustfinger for himself.

"Exactly as I imagined him," cried Fenoglio as he started to push his way through the crowd toward Dustfinger.

"Hey! Where are you going?!" Mo yelled. "He doesn't want to meet you!"

But Fenoglio wouldn't listen. He pushed forward. Startled, Dustfinger panicked and backed away.

"What is he afraid of?" asked Fenoglio. "Not of me, I hope."

"Of the end of the book," replied Mo.

"Because he dies?" asked Fenoglio.

"No," sighed Mo. "Because he didn't want to know what happens."

But Dustfinger had heard every word. "You think I care what you wrote?!" Dustfinger shouted. "I am not a character, and you do not control my fate! If you did, I wouldn't have wound up here! I'm going back. Now do you have a copy of the book or not?"

n his attic, Fenoglio tore open one dusty box after another. "The problem is it's been out of print for decades. And then there was a fire at the warehouse. I did hold onto a few copies, but then I loaned them to a book exhibition and they were stolen. I suppose Capricorn was behind the theft. Here we are!"

Fenoglio hadn't found a copy of the book. But he had found the original manuscript. Dustfinger grabbed the pages. "You'll do it right? You'll read me back in?" he asked Mo.

"I'll try. But not until I get my wife out," said Mo.

"Well then, we may have a little problem," Dustfinger said quietly. "You can't read her out. She's not in the book anymore. She's in Capricorn's village."

Mo was furious! But then he realized that while he might not need the book anymore, Dustfinger did. Dustfinger missed his family. He wanted to go home. Mo promised to read him back into *Inkheart* after they rescued Resa.

Meggie wanted to go with her father, but he refused to take her. Angry that she had been left behind, Meggie paced around her room. She stopped.

She could hear voices . . . whispering. She looked around. Peeking out of her bag was the copy of *The Wonderful Wizard of Oz*. When she picked up the book and opened it, she heard a witch's loud cackle. She decided to try reading aloud.

After a few minutes, a little black dog appeared out of nowhere. Meggie had read Toto out of the story!

Suddenly, there was a knock at her door. It was Fenoglio, but he wasn't alone. He had brought Capricorn's men with him.

They wanted to know where Mo was, but Meggie wouldn't tell them. Then Toto rushed out from under the bed and began to bark.

Fenoglio saw the dog. He saw the book. He couldn't help it. "She has her father's gift!" he burst out.

Basta smiled slowly. "Another Silvertongue! Capricorn will be so pleased," he said.

Meggie was going to Capricorn's village just as she'd wanted, but now she was going against her will.

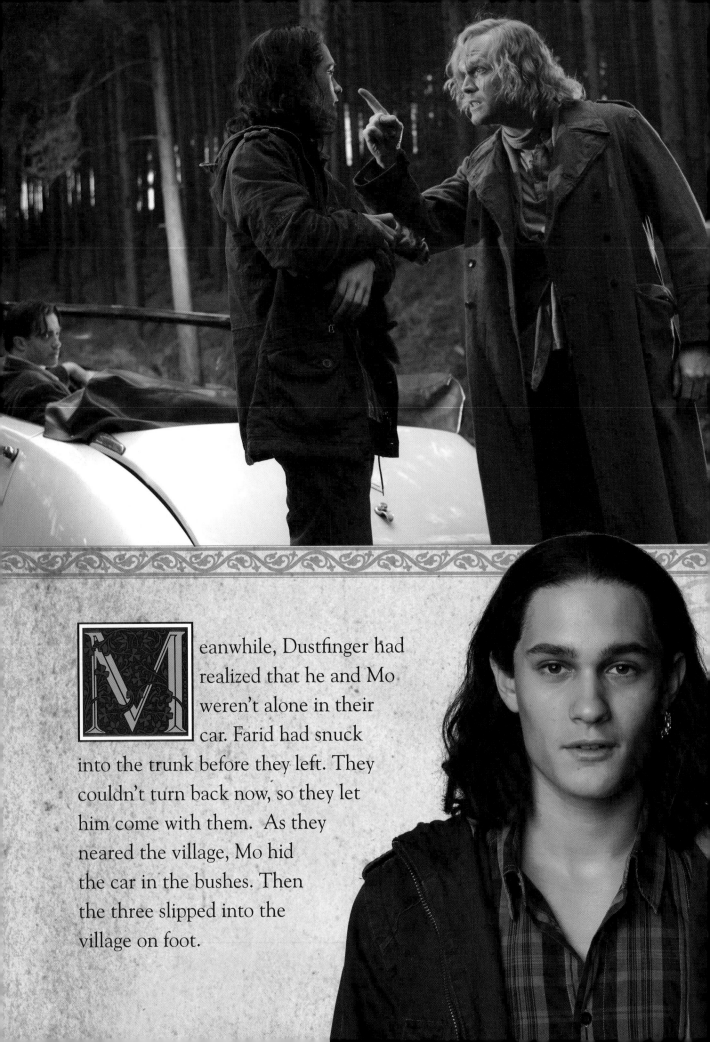

Meanwhile, Dustfinger had realized that he and Mo weren't alone in their car. Farid had snuck into the trunk before they left. They couldn't turn back now, so they let him come with them. As they neared the village, Mo hid the car in the bushes. Then the three slipped into the village on foot.

Farid led the way up a drain-
pipe and onto a roof of the maids'
quarters. While Mo searched for
Resa, Dustfinger and Farid stood
watch. But Farid made a noise and
was overheard. Guards surrounded
Dustfinger and captured him—but
they didn't get Farid.

When Mo returned, Farid was
terrified. "They're going to kill
Dustfinger," he cried.

Flatnose couldn't help but smile as he led Meggie toward the castle. "I wonder what Capricorn will make you read," he said to Meggie. "I hope it's something good. I'm excited, aren't you?"

Meggie was far from excited. She was tired and fed up with Flatnose, with all of Capricorn's men, and the entire adventure. She just wanted to be home with her mother and Mo.

At first, Fenoglio was excited to go to the castle and to meet the characters he had created. But after a little while, and some rough words from Cockerel, even he began to wonder if this adventure was such a good idea.

 nside the castle, Capricorn made Meggie read from a large stack of books before he was convinced. Now he wanted her to read The Shadow out of *Inkheart*.

Meggie protested, "You can't bring it out of the book! You burned the last copy! I saw you do it!"

But Capricorn had one more copy that he kept under lock and key, guarded by poisonous snakes. However, Meggie refused to read. "Let me show you what happens to those who disobey me around here," Capricorn said.

He led Meggie outside and pointed up. High above them, dangling in a net, was Resa. As soon as Meggie saw her mother, she ran to her. "It's you. It's you. Don't worry, Mother. Mo is here, too, somewhere."

"Well, what good fortune!" cried Capricorn, realizing who Resa was. "Let me look at you . . . ah yes, I see a resemblance. Do you still think I can't convince you to read for me?"

eggie had no choice. She had to read now. But Fenoglio had a plan. He was going to rewrite the end of *Inkheart*. Fenoglio stayed up all night scribbling away. But he was too late. A servant named Mortola took Meggie away before Fenoglio could give her the page.

However, just as Meggie began to read, Fenoglio crumpled up his story and threw it to Toto. The little dog carried the paper to her. Meggie slipped it into the book.

As Meggie read, The Shadow began to form and follow her commands. But then Mortola spotted the crumpled page lying in the book.

She snatched it away before Meggie could finish. Just as Capricorn was about to order The Shadow to attack Resa, Mo appeared.

"Keep reading!" he yelled.

"I can't—there's nothing left to read!" Meggie cried.

"Then write!" he said, throwing her a pen. And that's what she did. She wrote the words on her arm and her legs, reading aloud as she went.

" 'The Shadow reached for him with ashen hands, and as it did, Capricorn began to crackle and fade like the old page of a book, growing transparent and thin as paper. Capricorn's ink-black soul filled with terror as he saw the end was near.

nd so, too, did all the souls of all those within The Shadow's gaze who had committed villainy in Capricorn's name! And they all blew away—like ashes in the wind! While the terrible monster himself, disintegrated, and was no more!' "

Though The Shadow and Capricorn were history, Meggie's story wasn't quite finished.

" 'The Old Creator finally got his wish, disappearing into the world he had only dreamed of . . .' " she wrote as Fenoglio shimmered and disappeared.

" 'Finally, after what was almost a lifetime of wishing, the young girl's most heartfelt dream came true, as the mother she always knew she'd see again and the father she cherished came running to embrace their only daughter.' " Meggie dropped the pen; her story was done.

As Capricorn's castle burst into flames and crumbled to the ground, Meggie hugged her parents.

ustfinger watched the happy scene. Now he could never go home. But Farid had a surprise for him: He'd stolen a copy of *Inkheart*. Just then Mo walked up to them. He held out his hand for the book.

He began to read, " 'It had been many years since Dustfinger had set eyes on the wheat fields and the old windmill, but it was even more beautiful . . .' "

Dustfinger vanished. Mo closed the book and smiled.

Meggie approached Farid. "You can stay with us," she said. And the four of them turned and began to walk home.